THERE NEVER WAS
A ONCE UPON A TIME

THERE NEVER WAS
A ONCE UPON A TIME

BY

CARMEN NARANJO

TRANSLATED BY

LINDA BRITT

LATIN AMERICAN LITERARY REVIEW PRESS
SERIES: DISCOVERIES
PITTSBURGH, PENNSYLVANIA

YVETTE E. MILLER, EDITOR

1989

The Latin American Literary Review Press publishes Latin American creative writing under the series title *Discoveries*, and critical works under the series title *Explorations*.

Library of Congress Cataloging-in-Publication Data

Naranjo, Carmen.
    [Nunca hubo alguna vez. English]
    There never was a once upon a time / by
    Carmen Naranjo:
    translated by Linda Britt.
        p. cm. -- (Discoveries)
    Translation of: Nunca hubo alguna vez.
    ISBN 0-935480-41-2
    I. Title. II. Series.
PQ7489.2.N3N8413   1989
863--dc20   89-12822
                                 CIP

Originally published in Spanish by:

    Editorial Universidad Estatal a Distancia [EUNED]
    San José, Costa Rica, 1984

There Never Was a Once Upon a Time may be ordered directly from the publisher:

    Latin American Literary Review Press
    2300 Palmer Street
    Pittsburgh, Pennsylvania 15218
    Tel (412) 351-1477
    Fax (412) 351-6831

This project is partially supported in part by grants from the Pennsylvania Council on the Arts, and the University of Maine at Farmington.

Table of Contents

Foreword...9

There Never Was a Once Upon a Time...............11

Eighteen Ways to Make a Square.....................17

It Happened That Day... 33

The Game That Is Only Played Once................37

Everybody Loves Clowns............................45

Maybe the Clock Played with Time...................51

When I Invented Butterflies..........................59

Old Cat Meets Young Cat............................67

Tell Me a Story... 73

Olo...79

Foreword

The narrative of Carmen Naranjo has been favorably compared with the writing of not only the best women writers of Costa Rica and Central America, but with that of the best writers, women and men, of all of Spanish America. Her novels and short story collections have been honored with the most prestigious literary prizes of her nation and her region.

Naranjo, who was born in Cartago, Costa Rica in 1931, has written prolifically. *There Never Was a Once Upon a Time* is her third collection of short fiction, published as *Nunca hubo alguna vez* in 1984 in Costa Rica. *Hoy es un largo día* (1974) and *Ondina* (1983) preceded it. *Otro rumbo para la rumba* (1989) is her most recent collection. Her writing include numerous volumes of poetry, among them *América* (1961), *Misa a oscuras* (1967) and *Mi guerrilla* (1984). She is probably best know for her novels, including *Los perros no ladraron* (1966), *Memorias de un hombre palabra* (1968), *Responso por el niño Juan Manuel* (1971), *Diario de una multitud* (1974) and *Sobrepunto* (1985).

There Never Was a Once Upon a Time is a departure from her other writings in its use of child and adolescent narrators. The narrated events in these stories mark steps toward maturity for the children, many of whom are entering adolescence, such as the girl in the title story who destroys her friend's bicycle by riding it into a bus and confronts the chilling reality that time cannot be turned back nor deeds be undone. This is a lesson adult readers have long since learned, and thus they react with nostalgia and shared pain to the girl's narration when she protests that her friend was wrong to proclaim that there never was a once upon a time since the two of them had once shared such a time.

Although it has been argued that children, by virtue of their innocence, offer an unbiased and therefore more transparent view of the action, the innocence ascribed to children is not inherent, but rather an attribute perceived by adults and projected into child characters by adult writers and readers. Children's narrations are indoreliable: totally true to their own view of things but unrelated to a "reality" perceived by others. Such viewpoints serve as transparent lenses only for the children's realities.

The narrations themselves are characterized by a seemingly disorganized childlike discourse, which the translation seeks to maintain. Often the sentences are long and complicated, composed of a series of independent and dependent clauses joined frequently and haphazardly by the conjunction "and." The syntax and the verb tenses, like the stories, are unpredictable. Thus Naranjo reproduces a sense of time that relies only on the present, the here and now in which these children dwell. Although they refer to past and future times, child narrators never clearly distinguish them from the current moment.

The narrator of "It Happened That Day" discovers, as do many of Naranjo's pre-adolescents, that appearances can be deceiving, and is forced to face a painful truth: "I learned that behind one reality there can be another," just as hidden in one layer of text there can be many others. Like the layers of narration that are peeled back one at a time to reveal deeper meanings within, Naranjo's texts present multiple realities, often through metaphor. For example, the narrator of "Everybody Loves Clowns" compares herself to garlic and to a lizard because they are camouflaged, while she disguises herself so that no one will see that she is a clown "like someone who doesn't realize that's what she is."

For Naranjo, the child narrators of her stories in *There Never Was a Once Upon a Time* offer a view of reality that is at times so magical that it becomes a new reality. The young heroine of "When I Invented Butterflies," Clotilde, sees in common, grayish stones a beauty not perceived by others, then transforms the pebbles into butterflies that will dwell in the space between the earth and the sky. The child is able to perceive and even create a reality that is inaccessible to adults without the help of the child narrator, skillfully created by Carmen Naranjo.

Linda Britt

There Never Was a Once Upon a Time

There never was a once upon a time, you told me that afternoon at nearly six o'clock, and I answered: you're a liar, there is always a once upon a time, today, yesterday, tomorrow, because time always has room for long agos.

Then I thought: that long-ago time is like creating the world. I mean, there was nothing, no city, no house, no family, no friends, nor your house, not even the bicycle that's so damned important to you. It's like inventing everything all over again, just like it, only with the audacity of someone who mistakenly thinks he's the inventor of everything that already exists. What nerve.

There is always a once upon a time when a door opens and someone with a rabbit's face appears. You appeared one time, that was a once upon a time, although you'd like to deny it now because you're furious with me and your rabbit's face is angry, very angry, so much so that you look more like a monkey.

Mom, when she's as furious as you are, tells me I'm mentally retarded, when she's sick of having them call to tell her that I'm not learning how to write because I write Betsom botsom, instead of that stupid Betty Botter bought some bitter batter. The only thing that's battered around here is me, mom does the battering with her fists and nagging and she even pinches me sometimes until I tell her the whole truth.

Don't get so mad, there's no reason, we all do stupid things at some time or another, and I promise I didn't mean to do it. If I call you rabbit-face, it's not that I'm making fun, I love rabbits and the way they wiggle their noses, like you do, just like you. That's right, act like you don't know what I'm talking about because you know very well that it's all true and once things were different and you even loved me.

You know, moving here really suited me. Where we lived before I had the reputation of being a problem-child and they thought mom was a bad mother. It wasn't my fault the stained-glass windows in the church got broken, anyway they were old and they were so dark you couldn't see anything inside. Mom told me she couldn't pay for the damages since she didn't have any money, which was true, back then she was making payments on the television set and twice they came threatening to take it away from her. And to get everyone off her back she told them: if this brat is guilty, well let her pay for it in jail, I'm not responsible for her when she goes out in the streets. And she got so mad she swore, you know the bad words that we say every day and unexpectedly, just because we feel like it, it turns out they're not nice words at all and they nickname you "dirty mouth", so that everyone knows, what a bunch of cowards, and you aren't even able to defend yourself.

And so we came here and I felt like I was born again and when they asked me what my name really was I wanted to answer Katia, like two tough girls from the other neighborhood, but I didn't dare because here everybody was named Karen, and me with the simple and ridiculous name of Josephine, which is so easily distorted into Josefine, Josedull, Cheapjose and Josefly, like you called me when you were giving me a ride on your bicycle, insisting that I learn how to ride it because you wanted to lend it to me whenever you didn't need it. Nothing but lies, now I know that, because you weren't sincere and deep inside I'm sorry I ever believed your boasting and became your victim.

But even though you told me there never was a once upon a time, I know for certain it wasn't easy for you to say that, because it hurt me with real pain when you didn't understand that there are things people do without meaning to, out of sheer bad luck, and the worst happens when you're hoping for the best, like when you go all out trying to draw a triangle and your teacher with the ogress-face tells you it's a rectangle and you can't figure out when and how the fourth line got there. That happened to me. I'm such an optimistic fool. I thought you would care about my torn blouse and the bump on my head that was bleeding. But no, you acted like you'd rather not know who I was.

And you had known me before, you with the face of a self-centered rabbit who only thinks about lettuce for himself and for all he cares everyone else can just drop dead from a lightning bolt, an exclusive, fulminating, lightning bolt, as my grandmother says, she who is exaggeration personified, and she insists that it's better to die all at once, just drop dead, when really it's very nice to die little by little and watch everyone's tears while you're on your death-bed with the pillows all fluffed up and you say farewell with last words that are all about embarking on that long voyage and never returning. Each Christmas my grandmother makes the same old speech, that we'll never be together again on a Christmas like this one, because she's getting weaker and with the asthma that makes her wheeze whenever it rains or it's hot or she catches a cold, she just may not make it through next July and its heavy, endless rains. My grandmother's day will come, but not this year, it's already October and she's still around, asthma and all.

I know you won't be interested, but I had already thought about what I would give you for my birthday, because I do things backwards, when I should be getting presents I do the giving, a taillight, a big one so that everyone could see where you were heading, all stuck up with your swelled head. Now I'm not going to give you anything, just because you say there never was a once upon a time and you treat me as if you never knew me, when I know very well that you love me and you even would have kissed me once if I hadn't moved my face away just in time, afraid of being tickled by your rabbit nose. Also because the taillight wouldn't be any use to you now.

And so that you'll know what happened, my side of it, the victim's version, I'm going to tell you all the details and present my own defense. The things that happened were predestined, because one is born a klutz and dies a klutz. I didn't want to ride the bike, I was happy to follow you on my roller skates, pretending I had a horn to beep and thinking I was hurtling along at the speed of a comet. You were the one who begged me to do it. Damn the day when I allowed you to talk me into it. I learned how to ride poorly, because you kept telling me I was great and you laughed at my struggles to keep my balance and at how I nearly killed myself every time I touched the brakes unexpectedly and they threw me on the ground and I ended up with more scrapes than I even would have wished on my teacher. When I told you, okay now, I'm not afraid any more, you even gave me a push, but you didn't know I had decided not to use those damned brakes that always threw me off as if the bike were a colt that hadn't been broken in yet. I managed to avoid, by swerving the handlebars, two cars that were stalking me like panthers, but the bus I just couldn't, it took up the whole street. I saw the driver, white as a ghost, yelling at me to get out of the way, but I couldn't, I swear to you I couldn't, I thought I was going to throw up. Then I hit the brakes, right in front of the bus, face to face, fractions of an inch away, and then, it was almost a miracle, my guardian angel is such an expeditious, efficient type, I was thrown up over those enormous wheels and I fell, like a ripe guava fruit, on the hood, which was burning hot. You remember what a sunny day it was, but no, you don't remember anything, ungrateful rabbit-face, because you only saw, like some self-centered ego maniac, your poor, very changed bike, with mangled handlebars and two wheels that looked like they had never been wheels at all. The lights and the mirror were nothing but a fistful of crystal fragments that even a tiny broom could have swept into a pile. The seat looked like rats had eaten it, but the springs were still trembling, they were the only fragments worth salvaging from what had been, in your personal history, the bike that Santa Claus brought you, after you had asked for it so many times and dreamed about it in so many dreams.

And when you arrived, while the people, the good people, were giving me smelling salts, soothing me and consoling me with how it was a miracle I was alive, you, teary-eyed rabbit-face, piece by piece you picked up all the useless fragments of your bicycle, and you turned around like an indignant, furious goose to tell me I never want to see you again in my whole life and forget that there ever was a once upon a time, because there never was. And when you said that, as if spitting it out, I could even feel your saliva splashing on my face.

I won't stop seeing you, rabbit of my hope, even though you cross to the other side of the street when you see me, even though you ignore me in the park, even though you treat me as if we never knew each other, even though you insist on showing me that there never was a once upon a time.

That's why I'm writing you this letter, you with the face disguised as a rabbit, because really you have nothing in common with rabbits, except for that huge flapping nose, and you don't even care if it can sniff or anything, I want to tell you, I want to confess to you that if you really want to know, the scrapes hurt, the bumps, the bloody nose, the tooth I lost, the front tooth that my mom says will cost thousands to replace so that people won't see that I'm the poorest of the poor, it all hurt. The truth is, what hurt the most was the bike, the unfortunate truth is that I was also proud of it and proud that between its owner and me there was once something like a once upon a time.

Eighteen Ways to Make a Square

Although no one would ever admit it, Pepe is certainly the most entertaining boy in the neighborhood. He is tirelessly inventive: even the most mundane thing inspires his genius. Never even waiting for an invitation, he's always the first with the best initiative, the most perfect plan of distraction, the most amusing game or the most difficult exploit that in the end inevitably results in a unique and happy adventure.

All his circumstances are favorable: he is the youngest of eleven boys, a whole football team, and his brothers laugh at his pranks and they're even accomplices or collaborators in whatever adventure he proposes. His parents worship him like a little devil, clever, intelligent, and capable of bringing light to everyone nearby. He lives in a big house, with a huge playroom where no one cares if he makes a racket or if the floor gets dirty. And that's nothing, because they also let him have two great big hunting dogs that follow him all day long and watch over him at night from the foot of the bed as he sleeps. They are inseparable from Pepe; they accompany him to school and then in the afternoon they are outside waiting for him. When they greet him, wagging their tails and standing on their hind legs, they're taller than he is, but they never knock him down. Then they lick his face and smile, showing their great fangs. Pepe has trained them so well they seem to guess his commands, they jump up and frighten you whenever he wants or greet you very courteously or rummage through your pockets or knock you down on the floor and sniff you all over, all according to the wishes of their master, Pepe himself, who just laughs at what they do and then he calls them by name, Power and State, so that they'll stop. I ask him why he gave them those names and he answers that they're political dogs, leaders of the rest. He insists that he actually wasn't the one who gave them their names, which they acquired at some convention for dogs from all over the country, street mutts and house dogs who found it very difficult to leave their homes and yards.

And when he feels like it, Pepe himself can bark perfectly, moving around on all fours and stirring up all the dogs of the neigborhood, including his own.

During the rainy season, when the rain never stops from sunrise to sunset, all the gang was sick with the flu, coughing and achy, feverish with watery eyes, and it was Pepe who sent a message with his dogs: Carlos I am in bed and bored don't you want to enter the contest to come up with eighteen ways to make a square it's easy think up as many ways as you can and on Saturday put them in this same envelope through the slot in my door. I've sent a message just like this to everybody and on Sunday I'll see who has won and as a prize the winner will get my collection of lead soldiers that I've lost interest in of course if I win I keep the soldiers.

At first I throw the paper down because with my headache I sure didn't feel like playing Pepe's games, but then I pick it up again, because there wasn't anything else to do. I'd already been through my books and finished all the crossword puzzles and mom had turned off the TV because my eyes had gotten puffy.

Eighteen ways to make a square, that wasn't so hard and it could be fun, even when the prize wasn't so great, most of the soldiers were missing arms or legs and the paint was peeling off, they couldn't stand up by themselves and had to be moved by hand, besides, who was to say the contest would be fair. Pepe, who was also a participant, was the only judge. However, I find myself intrigued by the challenge of finding the eighteen ways.

The square is a perfect figure, with four identical sides. Four equal lines joined at their initial and final points form a square, thus:

1)

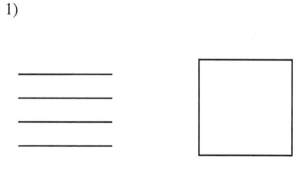

If you make one vertical line and one horizontal line the same length, and between them you draw a diagonal line to form a triangle, with another formed in the same way, united on the diagonal line, you will have a square:

2)

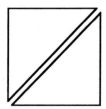

I come up with these two solutions very easily, so easily that instead of having fun the truth is I was getting bored.

Then it occurs to me that instead of writing, I should just draw. Draw what? I think of the easiest solution, to cut up a square and divide it in different ways, like this:

3)   4)

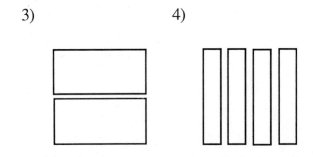

5)

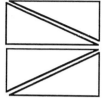

6)

7)

8)

9)

10)

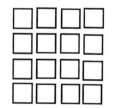

11)

12)

13)

14)

15)

16)

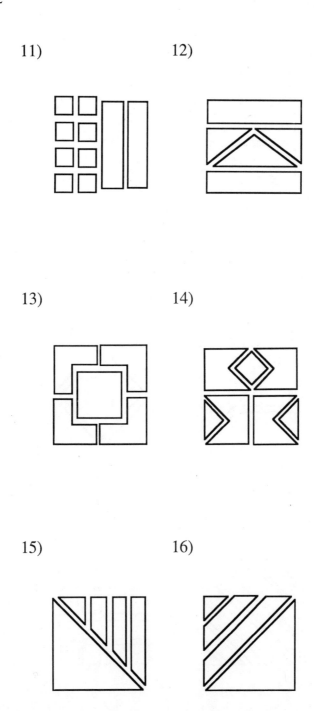

17)　　　　　18)

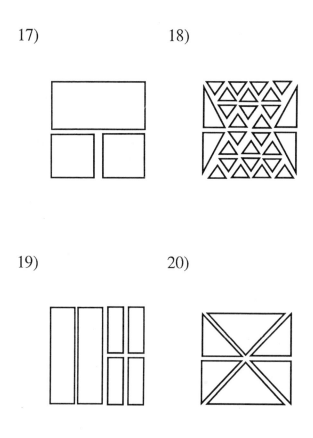

19)　　　　　20)

I came up with the twenty ways so fast, without even exploring the possibilities of the points, lines and

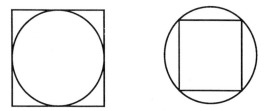

circles that were now flashing before my eyes, that I begin to suspect I haven't understood what Pepe's contest is all about, the trick couldn't be so trivial; there must be something difficult about it. Mom, mom, can you do me a little favor, call Pepe, 21-1881, and ask him to explain all the details of the contest he is organizing. But Carlos, you don't go in for this sort of thing, if you want to get better soon you have to treat your fever with lots of rest, so keep still. Pepe only causes trouble and nothing he comes up with is going to help you get better, instead it'll probably make you worse. Mom, you don't understand, Pepe is sick too and to help entertain us he's invented a game, one I can play in bed, it doesn't take any effort, but if I don't understand the rules I won't win and winning is important to me. Call him, please, and ask him if it's eighteen ways to make a geometrical square or a mental square. No, I will not call him, your association with Pepe isn't good for you whether you're sick or not, I don't like that world of strange communication he has with you, because even if today they're just boys' games, tomorrow they might be mafia deals and dirty tricks. Everyone is his own man and he shouldn't be part of a group, because that's where he'll get lost. If you're not an individual, then you're nobody, and I don't want to see you mixed in with all the rest. Mom, I only need to know what the rules are, that's all, what does it hurt you to call him and ask, please, please. I don't want to, I don't like Pepe, I don't like his dogs, I don't like his noisy family.

And I don't insist, what for, when she starts with the gossip and the rumors she turns into a complete witch, because sometimes she is only an incomplete witch and then she seems like the mom you have in your imagination and she is the mom we all love.

I manage to convince my little sister, who doesn't want to help at first because it's raining and it's too much trouble, but finally she agrees because she's hoping I'll win the contest and give her half the soldiers. I wait for an eternity and she finally comes back with the news that I'll receive a message through Power and State in the morning because if I send them out tonight they'll catch a cold. You see, he is more considerate than you are, besides he had a great room with tons of pictures, and street lights and traffic signs, stop and one-way and caution: dangerous curve. And you know what? His mom let me in without even blinking when I told her I was there for you, they let Pepe do anything he wants and his family might as well be his own little gang.

Well, now I was going to have to wait all night and that made me mad because if I could have gotten the rules I would have made progress toward the solutions. The night helps you think clearly, it has a strange way of opening closed doors. I try to go to sleep, impatient, restless, my hot flashes go away and I'm cold, I finally drift off and then I dream that the squares are made of jello, and they dissolve, the lines run into each other, smearing everywhere, and everything turns into clouds, heavy and dark and dirty.

Power and State come very early, I open the window, it's raining, the paper's getting wet and the dogs too. It says: you idiot of course it's a mental square geometric ones are totally unimportant and remember that today is Saturday and I'm judging the contest on Sunday your dear friend Pepe.

Aha; the mental square applies to a number of different cases and situations, when we went on that two-hour bus ride we came to the conclusion that we all at some time or another become squares, with no hope for escape, facing circumstances that weaken and trap us. What cases can we cite? I can't remember now. I pretend I'm on the bus again to remember it all. I had my bookbag, and I was wearing brown pants and a striped shirt. One teacher at the front, in the first row, another teacher in the rear, to watch us from every angle. Pepe was sad at first, because he had left Power and State behind. Later, when we were crossing the long bridge, he proposed that we play games; he would describe one and then I would do another.

Now I remember: first he told me how he became a mental square one day. It was in the street, a lady had asked him where the statue of Bolívar was and he didn't know the answer, but, totally self-confident, he assured her that it was in the center of the park that was two blocks to the left. She asked how old he was and he told her eleven years old, to which she responded that maybe after a few more years he might learn something, like how to read, the only monument in that park is the one to the Indian. And she looked at him as if he were the most ignorant boy in the world, he had never forgotten that look, when he remembered it even now he still felt totally humiliated.

Pepe told his story smiling, although he was sad and the words seemed to hurt him. That was the first time he mentioned the mental square. At another time he had said that Paco was a mental square because of the way he ate, he would eat everything he didn't like first and leave his favorite foods until last, without realizing he was running the risk of not being hungry any more when he got to the good part.

The essential ingredient in a mental square is the initial intention, which is so flawed that the error will eventually be discovered and leave us in the uncomfortable position of being fools, liars, useless or helpless.

With all these things clear, I took out my notebook:

1. You're a mental square when you don't plan your lie carefully enough and it's easily discovered.

2. When you exaggerate something so much people are suspicious and then the time comes to prove your claim and you can't.

3. When you make yourself out to be an expert about something you really don't understand at all.

4. When you fawn over something you don't like and then they give it to you.

5. When you hide so well they can't find you and you're still hidden when the game's over and they're playing some other game.

I'm thinking of the sixth and mom interrupts me with lunch: a soft-boiled egg with toast and jello. She asks me what I'm writing and I answer penmanship exercises to perfect my writing like my teacher recommended. I am creating a mental square, but this kind is very hard to describe. She thinks I have a fever and puts mentholatum on my chest. I eat everything very fast so she'll leave me in peace.

6. When you never tell anyone that certain things really get on your nerves and you keep putting up with them your whole life as if you liked them.

The seventh mental square gives me a lot of trouble, I can't think of anything. My little sister comes in with a how's it going and have you finished, and for whatever it's worth, I read her what I have and I assure her that it's only because I got tired that I haven't written the other twelve ways because I've already thought them up. Tell me, but I tell her to leave me alone, I want to sleep for a while.

7. When in front of the mirror, smiling and looking for your best profile, you start to think you're good-looking.

8. When they give you a compliment you don't deserve, you repeat it, and then you believe it.

And I fall asleep without wanting to because my eyes keep closing and I can't help it. At times eyes are just like the soldiers of our bodies, they make us obey the laws of the government even when it's not what we want.

I wake up again at four o'clock, and dad brings me tea with soda crackers and he asks me how I'm doing and if I'm getting bored. Well bored no, but I would prefer to feel better. He reads me a story, which seems very long and boring, although I am touched by his efforts to entertain me. Finally he leaves.

9. When you realize there's a trap and you fall into it because you're careless.

10. When they lay traps for you and you don't realize it.

Six o'clock, almost an hour it took me to think of two, and in my mind I go over the ridiculous things that have happened to me and to the others. They turn the lights off at nine o'clock at Pepe's house and my little sister isn't allowed out of the house after seven. I just won't participate, it's nothing but a joke anyway.

11. When they talk you into participating in a contest that's over before it begins.

12. When you occupy your time with things like this.

13. When you think of ways to make a mental square.

14. When you dress in the latest fashion with clothes that belonged to your brothers, who are ten years older than you.

The clock strikes seven-thirty, my sister has already been sent to bed and my parents check on me one more time before going to bed to watch T.V., it's raining cats and dogs outside and I still need four more mental squares, I give up, I know I am losing, not that there was any chance to win this contest anyway.

15. When you feel beaten because misfortune marks your destiny with constant defeat.

My stomach hurts and I feel like vomiting, I'm confused and I can't tell the difference between mental and spiritual squares.

16. When you decide to believe in a God that has the face of authority and keeps marking your grades down in his notebook.

It's already ten o'clock and Pepe's house is dark, it's rainy and wet, I'm disqualified, I can't turn in my envelope with the eighteen ways of making a mental square, but I am obsessed with getting the eighteen solutions and I only need two more.

17. When you think you're a window and you're only a wall, a big wall that won't let you see. (I am confused and I can't distinguish between beef and a cow; I think I'm very sick and I feel like a cow pretending to be beef, or perhaps I am a cow being beef, as in the game To Tell the Truth).

And it's eleven o'clock, and it's stormy outside, rain with thunder and lightning, and great big drops that make my room even colder.

18. When they praise you because you're a slug and you think it's because you're a star.

Finally I get to the end, the end of the end. The night is close and dark, with some luck I will only get a little wet if I run to put the envelope under Pepe's door.

When I wake up in the hospital, after hovering, they say, for several days somewhere between life and death, my little sister tells me I didn't win the prize, but I did get an honorable mention for the effort, because I am the perfect mental square of the neighborhood. I deserve it for being stupid, although it really doesn't matter any more, never again will I go along with Pepe's schemes, as mom says, if you're one of the gang, you stop being your own man and become somebody else's.

19. When you believe you are somebody for wanting to be like someone else.

It Happened That Day

Of course I remember, it was that day of the earthquake. At first it began slowly, as things were just moving a little, and afterwards it got stronger and faster until everything fell that was at all unsteady on its perch. I kept shaking for a long time after the earthquake stopped, with my knees wobbly, and if someone moved or a breeze stirred the wicker lamp, my heart went to my throat, and I was ready again to run anywhere at all.

Yes, it was that day when you showed me your collection of clippings, pictures of you as you wanted to be in the different stages of your life, dressed in a uniform with two long braids and straight hair, dressed as a bride with your white dress and a train covered with ruffles, dressed to go out shopping, dressed in a business suit in case you have to work, your whole life in that collection of pictures cut out of magazines. I asked how sometimes you could have blue eyes, at others green and still others the blackest of eyes, when yours are brown, and how were you going to arrange for your curly black hair to look blond, red, ash-brown and even platinum. You told me that's why you're a woman and women can fix themselves up in many different ways according to the circumstances. Haven't you noticed how your mother changes when she's expecting visitors, not to mention how she painstakingly makes sure the house is clean and neat (she even polishes the corners that normally never bother her), and she wears that house dress she saves for special occasions, and haven't you noticed how she puts on her make-up to go shopping and powders her nose when it's time for her to go to the doctor, and that's not all nor is it only your mom who does that, her friends have the same custom and one of them chooses the color of her eye shadow according to the dress she's wearing and she even has pink, of course I don't like that color and I'll never wear it.

And you showed me what you would be like on different occasions and we even got to pictures of you as a grandmother with bluish-white hair, thin, no wrinkles or double chin, a lot like the grandmothers in movies but nowhere near what yours and mine look like.

And you wouldn't show me the last ones because you said they are secret and very private, so private that *I* only saw them when I cut and pasted them.

Yes, it was that day when everything shook so hard. Since you were more scared than I was and you didn't have the nerve to go up to your room, it suddenly occurred to me to go through your things although my heart was pounding, fearful that an aftershock would make me pay for my curiosity. But the temptation was too great. There was your album, just as you had left it, in the corner of the box where you keep your secret things. I went straight to the last pages and there you were, you stupid barbarian! in the coffin and sleeping, straight from the book *Snow White*, which someone had desecrated as the teacher said and she punished the whole class so that we would confess who it was and you, dog-face, you seemed the most indignant of all and you even cried because since the thief didn't confess, it looked like all of us were guilty, how shameful, you said, and I remember your voice was even trembling, you little hypocrite. And you really mutilated the book because besides the picture of Snow White in the coffin, you also cut out the one of the Prince when he kissed her and then after that there were figures of angels, little comfort because you'll never go to heaven. Fat chance! Now I know you steal, lie, and make everyone else look bad with no consideration at all for any living creature.

Yes, it was that day when you came crashing down for me, just like the big jar that broke, and so I went immediately home and told my dad everything, but he found your album of cut-out pictures very funny.

Then I learned that behind one reality there can be another and I didn't like that at all because I had always tried really hard to tell the truth, my truth, but later I thought you must be interesting because even daddy laughed at your idea of seeing yourself at different ages and even as an angel.

I didn't turn you in because I'm not a snitch, but I wouldn't play with you any more and you sent someone to find out why and I said with complete sincerity that you are bad company, a hypocrite and a thief. As if to say pretty-please, you returned a pencil to me that I had lost a long time ago and didn't even remember any more, but that didn't change the way I felt. And then you defended me that time when I got really mad about a bad grade the teacher gave me for the answer to a question that I had honestly understood to mean something else, and I looked you in the eye and told you the truth. You turned very red, not from shame but from rage because I didn't know enough to respect your privacy, your secrets, and you made me feel ashamed, like a worm. Then you made me your tormenter because that day of the earthquake I had gained control of your sacred things. That was also how I, too, fell from the pedestal and was shattered into little pieces.

But now I think maybe I need to make my own album of cut-outs to see what I want to be like from now on.

The Game That Is Only Played Once

Almost everybody has already finished the homework and here I am with the assignment hanging over my head, and not even knowing where to start. Rosa wrote about a cow that flies and made it convincing; Alejandro about a river that talks, I didn't like it much, but it wasn't so bad; Inés about a race horse that ended up pulling a wagon, just like a story I saw on TV; Joaquín about a dog that saved a boy and at the end everyone applauded. I'm going to tell my own story, even if no one believes me, of course I won't say who I am and I'll camouflage myself to make sure no one will be able to figure it out.

"It's very easy for them, her and him, to tell you, go in and cheer him up he needs you. Don't overdo it, or make him talk too much, just keep him company, tell him a few things and if he closes his eyes shut up and leave, don't make any noise. And the thing is in this house I'm already a real zero, no one asks me what I've been doing, or even if I finished my homework, and how I feel doesn't seem to matter to them. They don't say good morning when I get up, much less tell me good night when I go to bed. I cough and no one notices, and if I say my stomach hurts they don't worry about that either. They have forgotten that I have a head which they could maybe pass a hand over from time to time.

Alberto looks at me with strange eyes, those eyes he always puts on when he loses, eyes of pain and rage. The poor thing never learned how to lose and the thing is he goes all out in order to win. He looks at me that way and I ask him what he's thinking about. He always gives me the same answer: I'm concentrating on the game that is played just one time. And that game, what is it; I've never heard of it in my whole life. I'm inventing all the rules now and if you keep asking me questions I won't be able to finish because you distract me and the ideas get away from me along with the strength I need to keep all the parts separate.

I thought and thought until it hit me. That turkey is planning a new game of wits because he knows that kind of game makes me nervous, when they make a fool of you it's horrible and if you only play the game one time I'll be labeled a fool forever. At mealtime, I tell mom what Bert, the great trickster, said to me and she starts to cry with great sobs, then the humiliation he's planning for me does matter to her, I run and hug her skirt and I cry too, without tears, so that she'll notice that I'm intelligent, and I realize that her Betito has a few faults in spite of his favored status, and every chance he has he sets a trap for me, because I am his foolish and bratty little brother, who has to be brought down with a single blow anytime he starts thinking he's too big for his britches. I hear mom telling dad all about it and the two of them cry out loud. Of course, they can't be pleased that he always treats me like this, because that same Albert takes things, he's like what they call on the radio a pack-rat, he wants everything, I mean everything, for himself. He was that way when he snatched away from me the most beautiful butterfly that by some miracle I had managed to catch. Afterwards he said he was sorry, but always with that little smile he smiles when he gives me the ball but just for a little while, and then he really offended me. He showed up as if he were generosity in person and gave me a completely faded butterfly, it was a very dirty white one and so common he'd already had at least eighteen just like it. I told him no, thanks, to make damned sure he knew that I knew how to tell the difference.

And when she and he stop crying, they hug me and even kiss me, while I hold onto what I can of those hugs and kisses, squeezing in between them, grateful for the solidarity of those good people, putting on that certain orphaned air which is always highly profitable when they finally notice me, and I sit there absorbing Papa's cologne that smells like a man and Mom's perfume that smells like home. At the end of that outburst, they run to Betito's room, they leave me alone with the sensation of having my hands full, and I've also been known to play tricks because Alberto has his good side too and sometimes I ignore it as if it didn't exist. He is very brave, he has defended me plenty of times in the street and challenged whoever was laughing at me and calling me a vulgar four-eyes, what blessed fault is it of his, the little prick, that he's got poor eyesight. He's also smart, I can't deny it, he told me how to solve the problem of the two trains that leave at the same time, with the same cargo and the same speed and they arrive at different times, and the answer earned me the comments on my homework of very good and how is it that your mind goes blank during exams. And a

*totally blank mind it would be if Beto doesn't warn
me about the trick they're playing on me, the
business of proposing me as the leader of the
toughest little gang, which already has a challenge
pending with the hard-hitting gang who hangs out
around the corner. That corner you cross and you
never know what's going to hit you, 'cause then
you're in the poor district of the Aguantafilos who
today greet you politely, tomorrow they hit you and
the day after they rob you while they say to you
dippy middle-class prick making up that garbage
about money and influence because your kind always
ends up out of work. And in spite of his warnings, I
fell into the trap and they hit me again and again,
even though I was whimpering and I cried uncle over
and over. And you, Big Albert, you had to come out
to recover my ragged dignity, I wondered at your
strong voice, your raised hand, and the way you said
very loudly what goes for him goes for me too. They
beat you up too but you really gave it to them.*

*When mom patched up our scrapes, scolding us
for being troublemakers, I saw in her eyes that
admiration that she has for you because you are such
a little man and the better looking of the two of us,
because you ended up with all the handsome genes
from our grandparents. I have heard her, when after
looking through your notebooks, she asks you whose
is that lovely nose, whose that full, well-defined
mouth, whose body is that which grows sleeker every
day. She's never said that bull to me.*

*After the competition, I heard that you fainted
when you were winning because at the end you were
left lying on the field. I know you're a faker, but*

mom she really was scared, she jumped over the railing like a champion hurdler. Thank God she was wearing pants, if not, the spectacle of her skinny bones in broad daylight would have shamed us forever. And from there straight to the hospital, at times she doesn't have a clue as to how much you like playacting, so much that even now you refuse to give up your role as a sick person.

And what is the game like that you play just one time?

You answered me that it was very simple, you already understood the rules and the only skill required is to let yourself go. Then I thought it sounded like a sliding game and I felt better because I could practice for that with a pair of skates or with anything that slides. When I was about to ask you more, the nurse chased me out of the room because I was tiring you now.

That nurse of yours is really fat, and she walks around so clean she gives me the creeps, she never sweats and she doesn't smell like anything. She's like an empty doll, an ugly doll, there isn't anything pretty about her, and all she knows how to do is give orders, even to him and her, she tells them exactly what they should and shouldn't do.

Since they take you away and bring you back home in an ambulance, our friends and neighbors are saying that you're very sick, it's bad and you'll die soon. What a great actor you are, Albert, to fool all of them. Well yes he is very bad, he's got them all fooled just to entertain himself, and he has invented the game you play just one time and he's getting ready to play it, you'll see, he'll win it and then he'll be the champion as well as the inventor of the game. Albert can do anything. They look at me in disbelief as if I were a fool. And I ask you again about the game and you tell me that to play it you have to fill yourself with air, air in your ears, air in your hands, air in your mouth. This is starting to get difficult and I become obsessed with exercises to help me breathe deeply.

A little while ago the house was filled with people and more people. They were packed in like sardines, it looked like a party. They were waiting for something and so was I. Maybe this would be the day when the great Albert would give a demonstration of his game, but it didn't happen. The people waited and waited, and then, tired of nothing happening, they went away very discouraged.

Afterwards they wouldn't let me in the room, however, through the keyhole I saw you doing breathing exercises, really very strange, with snoring noises that were frightening. You looked pale and tired, that's what happens when you put so much into that game you play just one time.

Days later they bought you a whole new suit, just like the one for your first communion, which I inherited later for mine, the only things they bought new for me were the candle and the cord, yours was yellowed.

Today they made me get up early and they tell me to go to my grandmother's. They order me to dress up in my Sunday best and tell me not to worry, I don't have to go to school, they'll pick me up at twelve to go to a mass dedicated to little Albert, it *must be to pray for your good luck in that game you spent so much time inventing.*

The mass was very pretty, with lots of flowers and the whole school was there with very sad faces. Something gets into everyone, they're all crying and hugging and kissing. They come up to console me, patting me on the back.

Mom takes me by the hand in a parade that's been organized on the road to the cemetery. On Dad's arm is grandma, all dressed in black. I think about Beto, the bandit stayed at home alone, he must be about finished inventing his game."

And when I return to my only-child house, proud of the grade of excellent and the comment that the parents should be congratulated for the imagination of this child, it must be cultivated, nobody realizes that I do know Alberto, that he lives inside me and I am learning to breathe like he does, so that I can play the game that is only played once.

Everybody Loves Clowns

If they were to ask me about vegetables, the only possibility that might occur to me is garlic, which comes in clusters, wrapped up in its own gift paper that's a lot of trouble to remove, but I don't like garlic because it burns and it smells bad, it's sneaky; when I bite it I get hot flashes and I sweat out the bad luck of it being my turn to clean a messy kitchen.

If they meant animals, I would never think of monkeys or parrots, which are always cartoon characters because they like humans and imitate us, I don't think of them or of ducks, or swans, or mice, who end up talking in fables, or of dogs and cats, who are enemies because ever since birth they've been taught to hate and they never have a chance to figure out that being different deserves respect. I think instead about lizards, always so happy, so well camouflaged and yet you can still see them because they leave their tails out in the open, and they can fool us into thinking they're snakes or colored leaves blowing in the wind. The lizard that's coming toward me now, ever alert to the sound of something falling or moving, nervous and quick, she raises her head and looks around, curious and bold, she's so long that rapid movement isn't easy for her and you can catch her very easily just by grabbing her tail.

But it's the human beings, people like me, who ask me over and over, what are you going to be when you grow up. A nurse, I said once, because nurses don't ever have to get shots, it's their job to give them to everybody else; and they don't get sick because they have to take care of the sick people and they carry keys and keep all the sicknesses locked up in closets.

Not a nurse, my daughter, that's a very self-sacrificing profession; something nicer, happier, and I think of the lizard, oh to be able to move as gracefully, pull myself along, raise my head and believe I can see or at least sense everything, I'll bask in the sun for a while and then scurry to hide among the greenery, with my tail out like one more leaf, only thinner and shiny.

Let's play house, my grandmother proposes, sensing that nobody else wants to hear that story again she's been telling since last night about one of her friends, who appeared yesterday in the newspaper, dead. I say yes and we make tortillas from scratch, and she pinches off little bits of dough and eats them because poor grandma is always hungry and her cupboard is filled with sweets and pastries. What are you going to be when you grow up? A parader, grandma, I'll go out in the streets early in the morning and only go back home to bed late at night just to get up and go out again the next day, I'll ride buses and taxis so I won't get tired, and when I'm even bigger I'll buy a car and head out on a never-ending highway. And she looks at me over her glasses, what a preposterous life, all day long in the street, when will you eat?

Later my mom and I look at the magazine she bought at the supermarket, with ads for clothes in it for both of us. We browse through it slowly because these are very serious decisions, a dress lasts for a long time and if you don't like it and it doesn't look good on you, you still have to wear it and wear it until it's worn out. I am not about to choose one just to choose something, and I won't let anyone else pick one for me. That lizard is lucky, her dress lasts a lifetime, and it's the best one she could have since it fits her perfectly and it never even wrinkles. Daddy says I don't look good in clothes with ruffles, they make me look even skinnier and besides you can tell the ruffles are just there to take the place of what I'm missing. So I skip over the dresses with ruffles, although I think they're pretty and the girls who wear them look so cute.

Do you know what I'm going to do when I grow up? I'll own a store that sells everything, material, dresses, buttons, elastic, presents with ribbons, ice cream, candies, malteds, and every day I'll bring you a surprise, the first one will be a sun hat, a white straw hat with a blue ribbon. I'll only sell the ugly stuff, the stuff I don't like, and I'll keep everything else for myself.

And now I'm happy all over because my uncle Jaime just arrived, he always tells jokes and riddles, and gambols like a lamb, and falls down and gets back up as if it were nothing; he can tie trick knots, snatch playing cards out of thin air, take eggs out of your pockets and balance a ball on his finger for almost half an hour. Everybody laughs and daddy says he's a clown. Uncle Jaime is the person I love most in the world, besides he never asks me what I want to be when I grow up. Although when he's here I know exactly what I want to be, down deep inside I'm completely sure.

He helps me practice the trick of falling down and getting back up again as if it didn't hurt at all, but it still hurts my behind and he advises me to put my bottom down softly and land hard on my hands, making a great bang on the floor. He gives me some little playing cards, just my size, and I tell him I'm going to train a lizard to dance with me in my show.

Everybody loves my uncle, even my dad who doesn't like other people very much, he hates my grandma and every time she talks about leaving he says do you hear that Lord?, you pick the date and I'll take you.

He comes on Saturdays, we all eat together and there's always something special that Jaime likes, they don't care what anybody but Jaime really likes; they always give the rest of us whatever there happens to be. And Saturdays are more fun than Sundays just because he comes over, does the show and I help out.

Yes, I want to be a clown, you already are one answers mom but daddy explains that there's no such thing as a girl clown, nobody hires women to be clowns because they're clowns to begin with, they paint themselves and they always wear costumes, no one will pay to see them because they can be seen for free out on the streets and in the parks. I feel like throwing an enormous tantrum, but instead of getting furious I feel very sad and I wish I were a lizard in my own little world, with nobody to tell me I had to be something else.

Well, since I can't be a female clown, I'll be a male clown. And I practice and practice with some old pants my cousin gave me. I put some huge patches on them, and I wear them with one of daddy's shirts and some spike-heeled shoes that mom doesn't wear any more because they're out of style. I fall down and get up again without getting hurt, well maybe a little.

When the word gets to my house that I'm putting on shows, I say it must be someone else and I tell a joke, sure that I'm camouflaging myself just like that lizard clown. They start scolding me, they're scolding me right now just like they were when that letter arrived from school with the lie that I've been disrupting classes because I keep clowning around but this time they didn't buy it when I tried to disguise myself like the lizard does.

Daddy furrows his brow, mom puts on her worried face, the same one she gets when there's not enough money, grandma sits very still, although she keeps moving her jaws because she's struggling with a big piece of candy, she's so impatient she doesn't understand the delicious pleasure of sucking it little by little and feeling how it slowly, slowly gets smaller.

What you've done is really stupid and it hurts us, you are very inconsiderate, making fun of us with your shows and this business of clowning around in school. We're not going to punish you and we're not going to forbid you to do anything, it's been a long time since you've listened to anything we've said to you anyway, you've just ignored our advice and warnings. We've decided to treat you the same way you treat us to see if maybe then you'll understand.

I think well, it wasn't so bad. I already said that everybody loves clowns. They don't scold me any more, that's what the psychologist advised them, they took me to her and she told me right away if you want to be a clown well be one all the time and then you'll see that nobody really loves clowns and people only put up with them for a little while.

No more scolding; no one talks to me, not even Uncle Jaime, who is becoming bitter, sad and quiet, and it's been a long time since he's come to our house on a Saturday. They never ask me anything, as if I didn't exist, and they don't even answer when I ask them something. So, it's a conspiracy. My grandmother's silence is the hardest of all to take because she's starting to forget everything, perhaps any day now she won't even know who I am.

I begin to feel bad in my clown suit, very bad, and it starts to bother me that they call me lizard at school, and enough I said one day in front of the mirror. Finally I learned. I wash my face, I brush the powder off my ears and my hair, and put on my white shoes that go with the blue stockings, my pleated skirt with blue and white checks, and my baby-blue organdy blouse.

Now they talk to me again and grandma didn't forget me after all, they laugh and smile with me. And when they ask me what I'm going to be when I grow up, I answer that I'll be whatever they want.

And to make sure they'll really love me, I have settled for being a clown disguised as someone who doesn't realize that's what she is.

Maybe the Clock Played with Time

Yesterday they thought it was just a dream, and I still think there was too much coincidence in the way things appeared one after another in the most calculated but totally unexpected manner. There were five that weren't great, but passable, who struck the tone and even managed a rhythm, without much style, without making anyone stop to listen, and without inspiring anyone to dance along with the music. All of them listened to records, but records don't pick up the problems of rehearsals, mistakes and out-of-tune instruments; things aren't always what they seem.

They knew what they were missing, some strings, some wind instruments, a little percussion and a lot of harmony; each musician retreated into his or her own ear and didn't hear the others.

One day they saw a moving van, and among the dressers, chairs and tables was an entire percussion outfit, with drums, cymbals and kettledrums. They went clanging along while the truck climbed the hill, the one with the road that kept getting more and more holes eaten in it by the rain and the sun. They all watched the movements of two adults, two servants and four children, until they discovered you, Pancho, almost at dusk, listening to a record blaring and improvising an accompaniment that at times was too fast and at others too slow for the music, but doing whatever possible to use the resources within your reach. When you finished, exhausted from trying to stay with the beat, they knocked on your window and dear Pancho they recited an inventory to you of what they already had: a repertoire of two flutes and one voice that imitated the violin and another that whistled very low until his two front teeth fell out and now his whistles sound like maracas with holes in them. And you, Pancho, open to new pastimes, and on saying pastime I thought about the clock and about my problem, you said that yes, you would join the band, that was just what you needed in order to see if you would be able to control your tendency to get carried away.

Then they saw the guitars being delivered, two of them, gift-wrapped, for the white house where the two little girls lived, all stuck up and smelling like expensive bath soap, and with freckles so red they made you feel horribly like connecting the dots as if they were the key points on a map that corresponded to an island surrounded by waters.

They approached the girls when the bus left them at the door where the servant was waiting, with instructions that they weren't to get dirty, to make sure they went inside right away. They told the girls about the band so fast that afterwards they weren't sure either one had understood. But they said yes. One, the whitest one with the points of a cosmic map, said that she could already play one song, and the other, with a red-headed voice, assured that she could do scales in the keys of la and sol.

The day they least expected it they saw Irene, with an instrument bigger than she was, going to her class to master the cello because her mom had determined that the sounds of that martyr were the most harmonious in the world and she had to find them, all of which turned into a nightmare just like math and geography, and she agreed to join the band as long as someone else would play her instrument and she could try the harp, which was her passion. They accepted the loan of the cello and agreed to look for a harp, which they might find given the invasion of instruments that was stirring up the neighborhood.

They found the boy with the dulzaina playing it next to the cornfield planted by his father, who had told him to come take care of it every afternoon and to play a little tune so that the corn would grow sweet and abundant, as things grow harmoniously and easily in the conspiracy of useful generosity. He said yes and he agreed to join the band, his name is Miguel and it occurred to them to call him Maiquel the Great. He always was the only one in the band who could carry a tune.

Later they saw two clarinets arrive for the house where there was just one kid, an only child, but he had a father who played in the Symphony. They called him on the telephone and explained the details to him. He said he'd have to consult his maestro and then they crossed him off their list.

There were already about ten of them when they saw a truck deliver a piano for the boy named Mauricio. He told us that his rich aunt had sent it to him, because I have a good ear and perhaps I'll catch on to what they call rhythm and I can invent something like what might be called neo-merengue. We talk and he complicates our lives, he assured us that the piano was an obsolete instrument, a simple decoration, what's today and important are the electronic instruments, the ones that synthesize and concretize. When he told us that, it was like divorcing us from our dream and in truth he divorced us even from ourselves. The dream seemed ancient, the band behind the times, foolish, old-fashioned, stupidly out of date.

We call everyone else on the phone, even the girls with the red freckles and the map-faces, to tell them that the idea for the band had fallen apart because it needed modernization, we had to bring it into the twentieth century. Wait and see what happens, and everyone waited.

Mauri gave us lots of lessons, but we didn't learn much because it was all theory, not practice, besides, although the trucks kept arriving, at times to take furniture away and at others to bring more, they never came with the instruments that we needed. The moment arrived when we got bored and we stopped getting together. We were left with a sort of void forever.

It was at that moment when my problem became evident, that problem that was always stepping on my feet, keeping me behind in everything, it made me useless when I was most needed, it made me go more and more slowly when I needed to run.

At first I thought that the clock in the main room, with its pendulum and its noise of a frightened heart, liked to play with time. It was striking two when it hardly should have been ten o'clock, or eleven, and me without sleeping, my eyes wide open. Afterwards I had the sensation that the same thing was happening to mom's clock, since she screamed whenever she looked at it that it was late, too late, she turned pale and the first thing she grabbed fell apart. The only clock that wasn't playing with time now, I thought, was the one with the bells, it stayed put at two in the morning or two in the afternoon, who knows why.

But later I thought the same thing was happening to me with time that had happened with the band. Everything seemed opportune, favorable, but the discovery that we were obsolete kept us from living the experience and trying to express ourselves with the music, if only to prove that perhaps together we could manage, with some luck, to play an entire melody. But nothing, our knowledge spoiled the effort.

Then I put myself inside the clock to find out how it was playing with time. The music of the clock is at first like a variation of the always the same, but it really only plays at consistency because each tick-tock is different, at times you hear it and suddenly it sounds so loud that it's focusing on you and it seems to pierce right through you, you can't do anything but keep listening and the sound gets in your heart and in your breathing, when you catch its rhythm you start choking and you even feel like you're beginning to be strangled while in your head it reverberates and throbs. It occurs to you to look at the time to see how long the invasion has lasted and hardly a minute has passed, one minimal and miserable minute.

I couldn't understand it. The ever-present clock, always accusing, sometimes for being early, sometimes late, and when it was naturally silent, almost sad from going along unnoticed, without reproaches, without questions, without hounding you

with what the devil were you doing, why so
inconsiderate and if you don't respect the hours of the
day everything falls apart because the train left on the
dot and no one waits for you, people have their
itinerary and if you didn't get there on time well the
hell with you. And you see the clocks when they
accuse us, when we don't realize that they're
advancing crazily and not slowing down, at times
they run faster and at others they go slowly, whatever
they feel like, and like a slave you look and see what
time it is, without knowing why it's that time and
not some other time.

My clock, that pendulum clock, always plays
with the hours of lunchtime and dinner, and they call
me because it's twelve o'clock and I'm not even
hungry, but they don't call me when I can hardly
stand it at about four o'clock and I'm thinking about
all the good stuff in a big salad. And it plays more
than ever when I go to bed and I realize that I never
finished what I was supposed to do on Monday and
it's already Friday, I'm sorry for wanting to play with
time even though it's time that plays with me, and I
can't understand it and therefore I go along changing a
schedule that someone else completed without my
presence and against my will.

But I'm mistaken, totally mistaken, time is
independent and I'm the dependent one, above all on
time itself. And it doesn't play at all, I invent the
games with it and I always lose.

The worst thing that's happening to me is that
mom and dad, especially mom, want to give me a
clock for Christmas, I know because I've seen them
look at me watching the pendulum and following its

rhythm. They'll give me one, I'm sure. She says a cheap one, but he replies good so that he'll discover the value of time, she asserts that I still don't know how to take care of things, he answers that I should learn, she that there are other ways of teaching me, he that this could be one, she that perhaps it's a lost cause, he insists on a good one so that it won't fail him because you and I fail him every day. And I answer them that it won't fail me even if it gains or loses time, because I'm the one who fails, just like with the band, because my name is Mauricio and I have a piano for decoration only.

When I Invented Butterflies

I kissed her on the cheek; I finally conquered my
fear and my virginity, just in time, because Nicholas
had not only already held Ana's hand, but he had also
kissed her ear, told her she was pretty, and she had
smiled. I closed my eyes, waiting for the slap, it was
better not to see it coming, but nothing happened. I
supposed that Clotilde would be furious, but when I
opened my eyes she seemed withdrawn, distracted, as
if she were dreaming or maybe thinking about
something very profound. Perhaps that's the way
women get when you kiss them or perhaps she didn't
even realize I had kissed her.

Then you shook your tousled bangs and you told
me, as if waking from a dream: of course, I'll make
them out of little stones because they are pretty and
shouldn't be quite so still, anyway they have a right
to fly and to have their grayness dissolve into colors.

I thought you were playing games with me,
speaking in riddles, since that's one way you hide
your emotions. Whenever you concentrate so much
on what you're holding in your hands, your cheeks
turn pink and your eyes water. That happens to you
when we're doing our homework together and you get
upset about a problem you can't get right, or we're
supposed to write up an exercise about our family
lives and I tell you not to write the truth but instead
write what they want to hear, that your parents never
fight, that they love each other very much, that
everything's going along just perfectly and you adore
your brothers, but you, Clo, you take it into your

head to write that there are problems, real problems that you don't understand but they are serious and at least once a month your dad packs his suitcases and swears he'll never be seen again and then everyone cries and yells and things get broken. And the same thing happens every time, they call your home and set up a meeting with your parents, which always ends up with you being punished for telling family secrets.

And you ask me with your innocent, shining eyes: Do you truly believe God invented everything that exists in heaven and earth? Of course, it had to be someone and that someone was God. And, He didn't leave room to invent anything, something new, something that will have a new life and dwell in the space between heaven and earth? I answer you, no, everything has already been invented, and then I suggest we go to the park to play ball, so I can watch you throw it softly, lovingly, and with that joy on your face that is so hard to find, my dear Cloti.

We go to the park, but you don't throw me the ball, you prefer to pick up stones and you confess to me that you want to invent something new, something like butterflies. You tell me: imagine the happiness God felt when He created them, how they clambered, daringly, all over His head and made Him sneeze, and how He thought this was a delightful game of lights and colors that would irritate evil men but bring only pleasure to the good ones.

And I bring you down from the clouds, because butterflies have already been created, God created them and He made them come from ugliness because first they were worms, horrible, disgusting, frightening worms, and they are only beautiful for a moment. You are silent, Clotilde, for quite a while and you turn within yourself again while you caress the stones. Then I suggest we go see what movie is on in case we can see it together later, and I don't say it out loud but I think about trying during the most interesting part of the movie to hold your hand, and about then hearing you smile inside which is how you like to smile when you're happy.

We get to the theater and you ask me if God also made the building and the movie. Of course not, but He created the human brain with the capacity for creation and so man can make secondary things all the time, but not fundamental things like the earth, the stars, the sky, and everything else in his universe.

I'm sure Clo goes overboard too much, thinks about things too much and gets obsessive; I wouldn't find it strange if she were to get up in the middle of the night and sleepwalk to find out where she could acquire some of God's power. I am a little frightened by her silences and by that way she has of entering her own little private world.

I kiss her a second time on the cheek, sure now she won't realize it, while Clo lowers her head to rest her brow on the shop window, and she contemplates the stones in the rings, bracelets, and necklaces that are sold in the downtown jewelry store. Doesn't it seem idiotic to you that people pay so much for these little stones while the others, the ones on river bottoms, in the parks, and out in the fields, the really pretty ones, are completely ignored? And I don't answer your question because you are busy inventing under those tousled bangs.

When it was exam time, I saw that you were pale and almost feverish, I knew you were studying like crazy because your parents didn't tolerate any bad grades, or even average ones. By that time I had already kissed you five times on each cheek and you still hadn't noticed.

I talked to Nicholas, man to man, to find out if those kisses were valid or if they didn't count at all in my efforts to lose my virginity. He answered me no, they didn't count, because when you're trying to become experienced in close encounters it's the response that matters and in the case of Cloti there was none; she wasn't even aware there had been an encounter. Even if there were a slight possibility that she was being very hypocritical and pretending not to feel what she was feeling, the only concrete evidence available was the very fact that she never let on she had felt anything. With any experience there should be an interaction and in your case there is none, except on your part, and that's too one-sided. I advise you to find someone else, Clo isn't the only girl, there is Cecilia, and Flora, or what about Tatiana; no one walks with them after school yet or carries their books or says goodbye a block before they get home.

Of the three he mentioned, I would prefer Ceci, although she wears braces and is kind of silly. For days and days I watched Cloti from a distance, but I still sensed her very near to me, still trying to invent what's already been invented. And I learned, sadly, that she did horribly on her exams, that they almost killed her at home and that her bangs had been combed back out of her face.

It wasn't until almost the beginning of the semester, when I went to register, that, standing together, we saw the list of the students who had passed on the very last attempt. There she was. She drew a red circle with butterfly wings around her name. You see, she told me, when I set out to do something, I do it.

As we walked out, I asked her what was new. I have a lot to tell you. I do too, and I thought about all I would tell her about Ceci to make her jealous. Do you want to meet in the park at three o'clock, as always?

As always, but what a baby Clo is, she hasn't even realized that it's been more than six months now since we've seen each other in the park, or even spoken, or since I kissed her on the cheek.

I wait for her in the park starting at two o'clock, and she arrives at three on the dot with a smile on her face, the first one I have ever seen. And what do you have to tell me? The most wonderful thing that will ever happen to me in my whole life, I finally invented a butterfly. You can't imagine what it's like, simply wonderful. I began with nothing but my faith, no tricks, just faith, I tossed the first stones into the wind and they fell again as stones, I tossed the second handful and the same thing, I threw the third with no results, but my faith was intact, I threw the fourth, the fifth and the sixth, now with doubts that started to nag, and the seventh I threw just to throw it, sure that nothing would happen, how was I going to work a miracle?, and I almost hurled the eighth just to get rid of it, I had no hope left. And what do you think happened? A little stone, the one that looked worm-eaten, the saddest, the most opaque, began to expand, to whirl, and it grew and it grew as if it were exploding from within, it was trembling, spinning all the threads of separate desires, along with the doubts and the faith, it was a terrifying frenzy, it seemed thrown into the middle of a family quarrel, until one wing popped out, with red, yellow and green spots and blue daggers, yet transparent, and another wing that looked just like the first, in colors and in shapes, now round, now triangular, now all in harmonic union. There, just when my creative imagination seemed totally extinguished. The two identical wings trembled in their longing to fly and in the center was the caterpillar, radiant now, so sleek, so colorful, and it started to rise, to dance in the air, it was enraptured with the light, and it fluttered above everything as if it were the lord of the space between heaven and earth.

I see you in all your beauty and I am ashamed of having kissed your cheeks when you were turned inward in the very act of creation. The bang has again fallen over your forehead, disheveled and blond. Your redness of cheek is also untidy, rather excessive near your nose and fainter in the corners near your eyes.

I ask you for one of the stones that you carry in your hands and I propose, out of your faith in miracles, to create another butterfly. You tell me yes, that with our faith, together we will make it fly. I throw it softly, not wanting to hurt it, and it almost doesn't descend at all, it begins to fly, yellow with deep-blue stars and brick-colored spots. I am at the point of not believing anything, but then I remember that I have created you, Clo of my fantasies, and that I kissed the air that surrounded your absent presence, because I had to conquer my virginity in the Clotildes that do not exist and I need to invent them so that I can kiss their cheeks without them realizing it during the long, solitary summers of my innocence.

Old Cat Meets Young Cat

Old Cat met Young Cat on a roof that didn't belong to either of them, that's why each one sat down on a cornice with a certain right of way that comes from nonchalantly walking on someone else's roof. Young Cat smiled at him. He was sociable and liked to have friends in many places. It's better to agree than to disagree; he had said that all his life.

Old Cat on the other hand was an old fart, he didn't even have many fleas because, to tell the truth, his blood was bitter and things had happened to him when he was very little, and even when he wasn't so little, terrible things.

An orphan since birth who had never known who his father was, he had to fend for himself from the very beginning, when he was a kitten with blue eyes and silky hair, before he could even say meow. When he was about a month old, someone crushed his tail and now he couldn't raise it even when a dog frightened him or he was challenged to a fight. At six months, because of a bothersome girlfriend who kept calling him day and night, he lost one of his blue eyes. With one ferocious scratch, his eye was closed forever. All that was left were his curled eyelashes and the appearance of a pirate.

His pug nose, with its two convex scars, spoke of defeats and victories, he hadn't always lost, because he sharpened his claws every chance he got. He had survived partly because his entertainment came from falling on top of his prey laterally, from the good-eyed side, and also because he knew how to play dead when his defeat had already been determined.

Old Cat wasn't bothered by sicknesses anymore, because he had had all of them: whooping cough, diphtheria, poisoning from eating a tainted rat, dysentery, laryngitis and one cold after another, besides pneumonia. And as if it were nothing at all, he was an expert in tolerating hunger, to the point that he had lost his taste for meat, milk, and cheese. Like hens, he had learned to scratch the ground and eat earthworms, he had learned to savor grass with the patience of cows, to kill flies as fast as any insecticide and to rummage through trash cans, savoring waste and the remains of fermented foods.

And in spite of his homeless life with none of the trappings, Old Cat shines healthy, even with his two ears eaten by mange, which he defeated when it was already running through his inner ear with a buzzing music he didn't like at all. In the process he lost pieces of ear and a little of his whole-cat appearance.

Old Cat did not return Young Cat's smile. It wouldn't do for Young Cat to see that he was missing his two front fangs.

Young Cat approached, smiling more openly and with a flirting movement of his tail that Old Cat admired with complete sincerity. He told him I want to be your friend, I like the experience that's written all over your body.

Flattery is a weapon that opens doors. Old Cat sighed, satisfied. In a bass voice, the voice that says o o o with cavernous echoes, without opening his muzzle very much so that the absence of so many teeth wouldn't be noticeable, he said what can a young cat so fine-looking and whose life is just beginning, and who obviously wants for nothing, want from me?

Young Cat really did have everything a cat can dream about: a home, a pretty owner who called him "treasure," a red collar complete with a silver bell, a feather pillow, canned food with vitamins, a nap in the yard while he hides the urge to chase the birds that hop from branch to branch in the trees, and scoldings because he rolls around in the grass to lose that bothersome odor of the talcum powder they put all over him every time they discover an agreeable and lively flea.

Well I'm interested in the freedom that shows in your every move, said Young Cat to Old Cat, I live well, but I'm used to always being clean and spoiled like a little plaything. I wish I could have your adventures, your wisdom, your life, which can be guessed from your scars.

Old Cat felt bad, very bad, like he might vomit. So his scars were visible. He with his only eye had looked at them with a feigned delight. He had arrived at the conclusion that the others didn't notice them and thought of him as just another cat.

But now this upstart was coming to confess to him that his life, which had been so unpleasant, was exposed so that any cat, even an effeminate and tidy one, could see it all and at a glance. How unpleasant it seemed to him that they could see him inside and out.

Old Cat answered that appearances deceive, they always deceive, young one, and on saying young one he adopted a professorial tone that made him puff up on his perch. Then he tried to be falsely modest and he spoke about the wisdom that the years don't bring, there are some old cats who are very stupid, wisdom comes from confronting life head on with a certain air of pride and a lot of courage.

That's what I want, shouted Young Cat, for you to tell me how to live like that, because I am just a stupid house cat, they haven't let me live or be a legitimate cat.

At that moment Old Cat understood his whole life, and he blinked his good eye, blue as the blue of the sky.

Little boy, he told him, everyone has a destiny and yours is to be a house cat, which isn't all bad if you think about the alternative, things can be very difficult, you don't know the statistics about how many cats want to be cats in a world overpopulated by street cats, vagabond cats, poet cats, artist cats, singer cats, sculptor cats, and cat cats. The world is screwed up because there's such a thing as hunger and every cat learns that one must be whatever kind of cat he can. Butchers sell us as if we were chickens or rabbits. There are those who say we are the hope for a white meat that is otherwise fast disappearing, and others who accuse us of causing allergies and carrying diseases. The politicians affirm that we are parasites and the economists predict that if we were to pay taxes, we could retire the foreign debt. We are, in truth, half useless, we don't plant, or preach, but we eat and take up space, pollute and use the love of whoever becomes enraptured by the gentleness of our origins as merciless beasts without piety.

Old Cat was startled by his own words, he didn't know he had so many of them and with such exactness of perspective. He became intoxicated in them and felt the need to say them, even if it meant his empty lower gum showed.

I can't give you any advice, I am just a simple old cat with my valid survival testimony. In spite of what I'm missing, I feel like a whole cat. And I know that whatever your destiny may be, sometime you'll turn to eternal questions: who am I and why am I here?

Young Cat stopped smiling and felt bitter, perhaps because his red velvet ribbon was choking him, perhaps because each time he moved, his little silver bell made him miss important words, perhaps because he had never discovered the blue moon that had formed blue puddles in that solitary blue eye, perhaps because that old cat was beginning to be unbearable.

The night, continued Old Cat, is my home, the home of all that is mine, because I shine in it, because I blend in with it, because I become its brother, because I wake up with it and stretch and feel younger and romp as in the longest hour, the one that extends my claws and my meows, the one that welcomes my complaints, the one that makes me invisible and powerful, the one that gives me keys to enter into everything, even into your stupid housecat corners.

Young Cat bristled his tail and meowed anxiously.

And if you have to choose, little one, choose the biggest, big cats love everything that's big, long naps, your own corner, absolute territory, a sunny patio, the rocking chair all to yourself, the silent bell tower, the patriot statue, the empty church, the solitary park, the abandoned hut, the ownerless cornice.

Young Cat attacked him with a single blow, and returned smiling to his feather pillow, there where someone was calling him treasure.

Old Cat, now recovering from the blow, entered with a bohemian air into the park of his nocturnal night. He came meowing the song of you look for me and you find me. He felt no pain, no sadness. With his heart happy, he confessed to himself that it is difficult to teach someone who does not want to learn.

Tell Me a Story

Tell me a story. I will tell you two, perhaps three at the same time. The first story you will know by its red color. The second is white and a third occurs to me that is tinted yellow. You should pay close attention so as not to lose the threads and then you can weave your story with my stories into a tapestry of almost three colors.

She was dressed in red that day, the red of sunsets and dawns, the red of ripe fruit and the red of flashing lights. She closed the door of her red-roofed house, she closed it slowly, carefully, to make sure it stayed closed. Inside were her treasures, her red book, her red coral necklace, her music box with red trim and the sounds of a red waltz. She was heading out into the world with all its horrible colors because from looking at herself so much in the mirror her eyes were red and her smile was red too. She was a red-head and she hid her hair in a dark kerchief. If she rubbed her hands together she produced an intense fire with reddish flames, that's why she liked rocks, which don't burn, they only turn a red and vibrant hot. She wasn't a witch, she didn't perform magic, although she liked to kill flies because they bothered her and wasps when they harassed her as if she were a piece of candy. That day she went out to take a walk, the sun was lovely, it wasn't too hot and it wouldn't burn, it just barely provided ample illumination for the houses, streets and horizons. She went out with the idea of meeting a new friend.

She, with her white dress, just like her shoes, had been out since early that morning. She had gone out for the purpose of buying white illusions and so she was carrying a little money in her white handbag. She really liked everything white very much, so she paused to watch slowly, very slowly, the white cars, white dogs, white houses, white linens. Her name is Whitey.

While Whitey crossed the street, Red neared the avenue.

He slowly pulled his yellow shirt on, yellow like his eyes. Today he felt more than a little lazy and didn't want to do anything, so slowly he took out his yellow pencils and drew suns, big yellow suns. If I had a dog, he thought, it would be yellow and I would name it Yellow. Then it occurred to him to go out and look for a yellow dog.

Red entered the park and sat down on a bench to think about what her friend would be like. A red friend who would like to play ping pong with red balls and paddles.

Whitey stopped at a shop window to see the white china on display and she didn't like it very much because most of the pieces had blue borders and others even had colored flowers.

He walked more than ten blocks without seeing a single dog, where in the devil had they gone, he only heard one muffled bark behind a door.

Whitey ran into Red, what bad taste she had with that ugly, shrieking color, how horrible all in white as if she were playing a faded angel.

The yellow dog was in the park, sniffing at things, ravenous.

He ran into Red, what a terrible yellow, he looks like an exploded egg. He didn't see her, he was going along with his eyes down, looking for yellow specks in the grey soil.

Red returned to the park because in the distance she saw a girl in a red skirt and blouse arriving, maybe she could be her friend. At that moment Whitey's white illusion was becoming more concrete.

He saw the yellow dog and admired its thin and abandoned beauty.

Red touched her shoulder and the girl smiled at her. Now everything was all right, this would be her friend.

That's what I'll do, Whitey said to herself, buy white paint and paint the fence around the house which until now was that really repugnant green color.

Yellow was tame and willing to follow him. He bought him buttered bread, while he was wagging his tail with all his thanks because his very thin body was not accustomed to that kind of good fortune.

Red played with the girl, who owned a red ball.

Whitey bought the paint and he took the dog to the park where two girls all in red were playing with a red ball. Whitey got tired carrying her package and she saw an empty bench in the park along with two red girls, a red ball and a yellow boy petting a yellow dog. What a jumble of bad taste! Sitting there, she closed her eyes and saw the white fence, completely white, purely white.

There the three of them were, when the red ball flew toward Whitey's head, and she immediately stood up and, without meaning to, hit the yellow boy.

What happened? There were shouts, excuses and the dog barked fearfully. Red said it wasn't anything, just a white girl and a yellow boy. But, I'm hurt, the boy said. Me too, said Whitey. And the dog licked Whitey's hands and then Red's. What an ugly dog. Don't be mean to him, he's my dog, what's so ugly about him. Whitey said he's ugly because he isn't white, while Red at the same time insisted that he's ugly because he isn't red. And after confessing their absolute preferences, with no room for alternatives, they were all quiet and a little embarassed.

Whitey, her cheeks pink and her eyes damp, said he wasn't that ugly, he had some very pretty white teeth. Red added that his red snout gave him a good-natured look.

The boy got very sad because they didn't like yellow, but he didn't think about how much he hated red and white.

Don't be sad, said Red, no, don't, added Whitey, what fault is it of yours that we don't like yellow? The boy asked her, and do you like red? I don't like it at all, it's horrible. Jeez, sniffed Red, what bad taste you have. I'm sure, Whitey defended herself, that you don't like white. Then they were all quiet.

Whitey took her package, ready to leave. Red said goodbye to the red girl. The boy called his yellow dog.

And, they never saw each other again? Who? The yellow boy, Whitey and Red. Of course, they saw each other a lot and spent some good times together. Something that happened that day, when one wanted a friend, another an illusion and still another a dog, got in through a hole in their heads, it's not at all pleasant to realize that for some we are agreeable and for others disagreeable. And what was it that got into them? I said got into and that's wrong, the correct description is came out. What came out? A little white, a little red, and some yellow, because do you know that when the boy washed the yellow dog it turned out to be white and when Whitey painted the fence it ended up pink and when Red looked in the mirror she saw that her eyes were yellow and her smile white.

Olo

It occurs to me to think that paradise, so sought after by everyone, is actually the absence of certain particularly aggravating inconveniences. For example: always having just one face, without any hope for change, and knowing that everyone else sees the same monotonous features, only now they're a little older; or for long periods of time not being the other or others we carry inside us, who only appear at times in our dreams with an identity that the rest of the world does not know and never will know, since we travel to our dream worlds alone, except for our fears, desires, faces, and aspirations, and thus we put on our most innocently conniving faces and we even play god, exiling our relatives, friends or enemies from life, and we also drop dead whenever a whim strikes us or when we have no other way out.

Or perhaps another: having to go to work, which has a nice patriotic ring to it and sounds fine in philosophical treatises or in economics books, but wears thin as a daily reality looked at honestly, rather than with that illusion of remuneration that paints our paydays with shopping sprees.

Less cruel, but equally oppressive, is the concrete limit to our dreams that appears and very quickly converts them into the invisible objects of an accustomed glance or into the mummies of a constant nightmare, in which they appear as figures refined in the cruel art of robbing us of space, light and air.

Paradise is somewhat like a voluntary flight to the nonexistence of the bothersome and the tedious, and therefore it is everything that isn't confining or corrosive, or tiresome, or inconvenient.

And there are as many paradises as there are people, and into them, with or without imagination, one puts everything that would otherwise escape in a metaphorical luster, like ideas from our infrequent leisure time when we can think freely, or maybe love, which is like a rite of passage to the naked reality where words are one more shroud that falls into the poetic inertia of feeling itself growing.

Men with imagination carry their lost paradise with them, with the sadness of great lords who have been dispossessed of their rightful lands.

Men without imagination have a forgotten paradise, because they simply do not dare to remember dreams, and in the everyday fuss they believe in measuring days as clocks mark time.

One and all feel a nostalgia, which at times brings on a depression and at others cheers them up, a nostalgia that helps them remember with delight the most unexpected places or feel like strangers in their own homes, their own streets, their own neighborhoods, or see in someone else's face a solidarity without kinship, or touch a communion of unconscious, identical distances, or verify differences between similar signs of a neighborhood promiscuously populated by jobs, properties and families.

I don't have a lost paradise nor a forgotten paradise because a part of me was born in Olo. But I do carry with me the pain of nostalgia that's been transformed into an instinct to return.

II

Olo has few residents, because one is born there only in pieces and throughout life those who are integrated into the Olototal all return. However, children, adolescents and old people live there because some have the magic of being and remaining Oloans.

Four mountain peaks signal the cardinal points and their shadows mark the hours of the day onto a valley of fresh green pasture, where it rains musically every night from seven until eight o'clock, when one is not fully awake but not yet asleep and the rain has a rhythm of rocking chairs and lullabies that stirs the memories of the musicality of mothers' cooing and cradle songs and the fascinating suggestion of a brook flowing toward the paternal river, and even farther to the changing blue bosom of the sea as serenely as a sailboat.

The people of Olo go to bed early and get up at dawn to see the entire sky covered with stars, and feel the immensity of space like an open hand that holds everything grand and everything intimate. When a light slides through the avenues of stars, just like the mischievous figure of an oil lamp in an orderly parade of electric lights, children, adolescents and old people understand the message that the sky teaches when it turns into a mirror and answers prayers. Then they contemplate the struggle of the dawns, and the red and orange lances illuminate their faces, where the elusive peace of birth can be found.

Each day in Olo is a new day, unrelated to a weekly inventory; all of time is full of nows and the value of later is unknown in the whistling language of the sincere.

Little paths of grass and flowers lead to the houses, which have neither doors nor keys. Small courtyards of irises and lilies or hyacinths and hydrangeas or poppies and daisies or dahlias and roses precede the hallways with their bannisters covered by climbing vines where bees buzz and hives hum. In the houses there are no cupboards or wine cellars, and no calendars; one has everything necessary to walk fearlessly, work tirelessly and live without the shadows of pyramids on backs bowed over, seeking the traces of lost images. A single bedroom houses the entire intimacy of the family, and in it family members eat and sleep, cook and read, reflect and grow in acts of love as pure as they are profound.

Disorderly frosts paint the leaves in the valley almost yellow in autumn, the pines and cypresses on the horizon remember the verticality of winter, branches of elm and fig trees sustain the perpetuity of spring and the summer stretches out with its hands overflowing above the golden prosperity of the grass.

Along a path that has ruts but is not dangerous, which crosses the lower rims of the mountain range, the Oloans go to the sea, singing verses of salt and sand. On the beaches they make bonfires and sing songs and rounds for ritual baptisms, marriages and farewells, for it is there they leave those who have abandoned the air and can no longer see the battles of dawn over the mountain peaks. They leave them, their arms by their sides, eyes open, and give them a cedar oar for their voyage to the maternal bosom of the water. The Oloans do not cry at farewells; they know that in the world's eternity death has its place. Several of them, the oldest ones, believe death is a prettier place than Olo and they get wrapped up in the rare nostalgia of the pilgrimage that needs to keep moving forward in its blind desire to hold onto the dawn.

Work in Olo means the profession to which one is called. Each Oloan does his own thing for himself and for everyone else, too. Every task has meaning. The children at play demolish the houses from that time when Olo was different. With the tenacity of sweaty work-days combined with mysterious rites that revolve around magic words, the bricks and wood disappear in a twinkling. The ruins are shrinking, and now all that remains of some of them is an empty stain in the grass.

III

One day a traveller arrived in Olo who kept marvelling at the beauty of the valley. The poor man had encountered a problem with the authorities of his own country; he told about the people there who believed in authority as a mission and in obedience as the destiny for everyone else, and about being exiled for not showing his complacency to one of the many measures that were taken by the people in power. The Oloans listened respectfully, without understanding anything he said, since the talk about orders, commands, armies, fear and decrees sounded to them like a foreign language. If it hadn't been for their faith in words, being inclined to believe in them as the real names of deeds, things, and people, they would have doubted the mental stability of the visitor.

After a while, having shared a house, food, and a job, he asked to be considered a citizen of Olo. These people had never heard of such a request; they simply thought themselves to be a part of that place, like the trees, the rivers, the mountains and the valley. They told him he should find citizenship for himself. But they were surprised when he asked where he could find the documents and before whom he should initiate the formalities. After mulling over that unknown language, the reply they gave him was that all the answers were within himself. The visitor then said that he already knew them and he was ready to earn the privilege of being a citizen of Olo.

Thus the problems began. As the people were working, the man began to teach them faster and easier ways of doing their jobs, but his new methods were so mechanical and monotonous that they didn't go with the beat of the songs nor permit the care necessary to avoid disturbing nature or hurting the animals. One Oloan, at the numbing insistence of the stranger's advice, lost a finger that had become entwined in the weeds he was cutting. Then the visitor changed his tactics and suggested that at dawn they should organize a neighborhood watch committee "with the purpose"—those were his words—"of safeguarding all properties." As no one understood his plans, there was no response and the man, who mistook the silence for assent, began the activities to recruit guards. The only volunteers he found were the children, who thought this was a new game to make the night last longer and surprise the dawn early. When they saw that the training obliged them to march in rows, throw their chests out and hold their breath, look all around with a suspicious gesture that frightened the butterflies, and to use slingshots and pebbles that startled the birds into flight, the children deserted without any explanation other than "we don't want to."

He thought that the exercise, even though it was small and isolated, had not been understood by the children. Of course, he said to himself, here they need the complete structure of a government and not just an isolated batallion of vigilance. That night his work kept him up late; he drew charts of authorities that shared a common head and were regulated by powers that dictated the laws or applied them, or who dedicated themselves to organizing an electoral process for the democratic selection of the head of state. The following day, he made even more charts and thus he managed to give public employment to the most recent Oloan and still there weren't enough Oloans for all the jobs, so he had to consolidate several positions into one. Full of enthusiasm, he wanted to communicate his great plans to the people, but prudently he thought about the necessity to finish first the task of revising the laws, statutes and regulations.

He spent more than a month on these projects, because the wording bothered him and he didn't want to leave any loopholes that would allow people to misinterpret the revisions later on. Tired, but feeling satisfied from having done his job well, the man called the Oloans together in the town square, which was decorated with sea pebbles and shells of all kinds.

Once assembled, they heard the elevated speech of the visitor, which started with his explanation regarding the need for government and then there was something about "of the people, for the people and by the people." They listened to him reading the principal laws and they saw the charts, which for some of them were too similar to the squares and rectangles they detested; by mutual, silent agreement in Olo the straight line and all its angles and vertices had been eliminated, and circles were all that remained.

With his voice hoarse, the man concluded by asking for the authority to establish the described organization, and only then, no longer blinded by the illusion that had inflamed his speech with convincing words, did he confirm that the Oloans had been distracted for quite a while watching the flocks of birds that were fluttering overhead. It was not easy to penetrate the ingenuous souls of the Oloans, who were devoted to the simple formation of nature.

The man thought that such a primitive organization needed more primitive elements. Sure that he had hit the nail on the head, he waited with renewed hope for the new dawn. Then, while the Oloans were watching the sky, he began to talk about a god within the curious context of magic. "He was what he wasn't until the ordaining force of the beginning stretched out in chains of causes and effects." The people were convinced that this man simply could not remain silent and he needed to speak just as they needed to eat. They let him talk until a child finally cried BORING.

The visitor, now desperate to establish himself, believed that his task must be performed solitarily in that strange place without governments or metaphysical preoccupations. Words and ideas were not convincing; he thought that perhaps they were stifled by the beauty and goodness of nature. Besides, men, in an ingenuous manner, tended toward great creations when a small one would do. Something productive and simple, he told himself and then repeated, sure this time he had hit the nail on the head. "Other people need to know about this place, they'll bring money in and they'll be fascinated by this clean air, this tranquility, even by the simple and original houses of the inhabitants."

He designed posters and bulletins and he wrote advertisements, but he wasn't happy with the simple and unadorned name of Olo. Convinced that denomination is essential in determining the matter and shape of things, he tried an initial h and was pleased by the interesting slant of the change. "Holo is certainly more distinguished." Not satisfied he added another h at the end, "Holoh is stupendous, strange, exotic." And the intermediate h stirred him from his complacency; finally he had achieved a sophisticated touch. He prepared more than one hundred signs for "Holhoh," with directions and arrows: "This way to Holhoh," "Welcome to Holhoh," "Holhoh straight ahead," "Visit Holhoh."

During the seven o'clock rain he placed the signs in a number of different locations. The following day, the Oloans very politely escorted him to the border and left him there, with the cordial request that he never return.

IV

I don't know all the Oloans, but I remember some. I seem to recall seeing the eldest seated among the trees, not because he was looking for shade but for the purpose of communing with the owners of that tall foliage. There in the solitude that whispers of leaves and branches, the old man hooked rugs with the virile gestures of an artist. Without a pattern, at the whim of the threads and stitches, he was tracing the sponginess of the stitching, and while he did it he was uttering the most brilliant thoughts in the grass. Anyone nearby could hear that voice reflecting wisely about the most profound and obscure things. When I asked him the why of his thoughts, he seemed not to remember what he had been thinking and he only showed me the unfinished arabesques of his stitches. Once when I insisted I met the cloudiness of tears in his eyes. Since that day I have respected his solitude among the trees.

There were two very good friends among the Oloans. Wherever one went the other followed, without knowing or even trying to figure out who was following whom. Together they cultivated a raspberry patch and together they shared their raspberries with everyone else without worrying about how many they kept for themselves. They always spoke in the generous plural of love. I remember them being very sad on the road to the sea. The other one wouldn't come back, he stayed on the beach, next to his brother's oar. The Oloans respected his pain as they had also respected the language of silences that had existed between the two.

The Oloan grandmother was very big. In her lap there was room for eight or more children. With short, unsteady steps, as slow as her stories about birds and flowers, she gathered dry sticks for her fire. She made pastries, cheese turnovers and sponge cakes. Grandmother loved me very much and when she saw me leave, she raised her hand as if it were a candle in the window awaiting my return. Upon arriving I will find her smiling and she will raise her hand with a gesture like a story in suspense.

I remember the kids who were in charge of collecting the honey from the hives without disturbing the bees. The plan was simple. First we gathered the most aromatic flowers and scattered them where the bees were looking for the thread for their alchemy. The novelty of the free, fertile field drew them in swarms away from the hive and then we could distill the honey without offending the bees, even though in Olo they weren't venomous. The precaution was a courtesy in homage to their rights as homeowners, since they had not yet learned to share their houses with others. With these children I went on great expeditions of apprenticeship. There were five of us and the mutual agreement in our games was a lesson in peaceful coexistence and respect, exactly when egotism was most alert and most impulsive in the ingenuousness of its demands. The distribution of lots and turns created a spiritual peace that left no room for resentment or temper; everyone was ready to give and receive without credit or dividends. And, neither competitive nor shy, my group reached out to others and we all blended happily together. The preference that prevailed everywhere was to enjoy the company and the moment; we were aware of playing an honest game where both victories and defeats were celebrated.

I remember too the women who were doing the wash in the rivers, as nakedly pretty as the water, the stones, and the moss. I seem to remember the men caring for the land, bent over the happiness of the young sprouts. They stood out among the rows of vegetables like itinerant bodies that generously donated their weariness to the task. Others in their shops or at their looms formed scenes of virile tenacity or of entertaining chores that agilely combined patience with skill.

I remember the frequent picnic lunches, where there was always dancing and singing over a music of murmurs and words.

I don't remember my Oloan parents, perhaps they didn't exist because they would have been too exclusively mine in a place where everything belonged to everyone.

V

The sad thing is that bad things also have their time and place.

It was on the beach, that day of the baptisms, when the seagulls flew up, frightened, as if they sensed the danger. A boat full of strangers traced lines of foam on the sea, which was becoming rough. They surrounded us with curious glances, inventorial looks that would fall later and forever after on top of me. They took photographs and they laughed a lot to see our nudity, so that we were ashamed and hid in the rocks. Then they tried to hunt us as if we were rabid animals.

I ended up in the midst of Skywalker, Earthwalker and Windwalker. My friends called me, called me...I still remember their voices; on clear, starry nights, they return again with a note of lament.

Skywalker needed to wander among the towers, to feel the distance between beings and things. The higher he climbed, the more the weight of his desire for greater heights made him lose his perspective. He never wanted to see from his own level, on the level of things that are approaching or leaving. He believed in a view from the heights that would synthesize and wrap up the world in one enormous sentence that would have repercussions for everyone, even when he was afraid of falling and had deliberately forgotten the immediacy he had felt when walking on level ground. He looked at me with a certain condescension and he was surprised to observe me so distant, a surprise that was converted into a schematic definition (that is his vocabulary) in order that he might elaborate it further in the future and classify me into a concept: "Primitive being that will evolve when incorporated into the culture." Poor Skywalker, I have learned little from him, except for the tragic lesson that heights are not reached on terraces or towers.

Earthwalker seemed more Oloan to me; I even started believing that he was living, as I was, a return life. He coveted everything that appeared in his path and he collected it all, because he was determined to trade the things he possessed for new things he saw. I began imitating him, with the conviction that there was some vital force in him aimed at expending itself for some sacred and valuable purpose. Earthwalker never failed to change whatever he found in his path, sometimes putting into it the zeal of his strength and vigor. Since the significance of the exchanges was lost on him, poor Earthwalker suffocated from the unnecessary objects he collected. The worst thing is that the only satisfaction he got out of his ambitious labor was in being able to show what he had to the other Earthwalkers, Skywalkers and Windwalkers. Once the objects were displayed, the illusion of his ownership dissipated and Earthwalker had to dedicate himself to collecting other things, especially if they belonged to a neighbor or relative. The difference between him and Skywalker was simple; Earthwalker never stopped looking at what was nearby and he got completely lost in his detailed analyses, so he never managed to go beyond his own inventory and that of the others. All I learned from him was that the plain was a large, absurd security blanket.

Windwalker was completely different. He denied reality and believed in dreams that come true. He wasn't worried about the everyday, certain that he would somehow achieve the unique, which he dreamed about with his eyes open, not even stretching his imagination. Games of chance, lotteries and luck were his preferred ways to travel. He bet on everything and therefore he was like an emigrant or a pilgrim, always on the trail of good winds. He smiled frequently, scaring off sadness, a very bad omen due to its piercing lances. He didn't believe in stability or in ceremony, but in the spontaneity of his dreams. Such indifference inspired me until I saw in

Windwalker's eyes the same symbols that existed in those of Skywalker and Earthwalker, merely disguised by his approach of doing things without even the least little effort.

All around were the combinations Skywalker-Windwalker, Windwalker-Earthwalker, Skywalker-Earthwalker, etcetera, etcetera, because there were infinite variations according to the extent of the influence of each.

I began to feel a great homesickness for Olo that led me to say the simplest things, like these:

VI

Olo is the prettiest place I know. There a part of me was born, only a part, a very small part surely. While Skywalker cries distances, Oloan lives proximities. When Earthwalker measures his exhaustion, Oloan again experiences the dawn. While Windwalker complains about so many borders, Oloan looks calmly at a world that is born in Olo through the mere effort of an extended hand.

In Olo there are no streets, or highways, or tall buildings, therefore it doesn't appear on the map nor do tourists visit it. Neither does it have churches, it hasn't occurred to anyone to build them, and thanks to their absence no one hears sermons or cites Biblical scriptures, hears confessions or doles out penances.

Olo is truly beautiful, there the old ones and the children aren't a bother to anyone, and what's more they play with each other and talk together in the plazas. I forgot to say that there is no museum, because Olo has no history, no culture, no tradition, no archives. Oloans live in Olo without memories, no one cares what happened yesterday, and what's truly incredible is there are no banks because nobody keeps anything and daily expenses make up the entire economic structure. Neither are there schools; everything good is learned in the gardens and nobody remembers the bad.

A very small part of me was born in that place, what a pity someone brought me here and introduced me to the Skywalkers and the Earthwalkers and the Windwalkers.

You ask me where Olo is. But you believe if I knew, I would still be here.